KU-094-659

This igloo book belongs to:

....

igloobooks

Published in 2015
by Igloo Books Ltd
Cottage Farm
Sywell
NN6 0BJ
www.igloobooks.com

Copyright © 2014 Igloo Books Ltd

All rights reserved. No part of this publication may be
reproduced or transmitted in any form or by any means,
electronic, or mechanical, including photocopying, recording,
or by any information storage and retrieval system,
without permission in writing from the publisher.

HUN001 0215
2 4 6 8 10 9 7 5 3 1
ISBN 978-1-78440-290-7

Illustrated by Julia Seal
Written by Melanie Joyce

Printed and manufactured in China

Fly, Freddy, Fly!

igloobooks

Freddy loved playing with his friends, Lenny and Flo.
They whizzed down the slope on a little, red sledge.

"Whee!"

cried Freddy.

Suddenly, the little sledge **swerved**.

It skidded... ...and flipped.

Everyone tumbled out into a tangle. It was the best fun, **ever!**

"Oops!" they all cried, bursting out laughing.

Freddy just loved playing in the snow.

Then, one morning, something was different.
Everyone was jumping about, as if they had fleas.

"Is it a new game?" asked Freddy.

"No. We're learning to fly!" replied Lenny and Flo.

"Come on, flap, flap!"

squawked the flying instructor,
wafting his wings.

"I can't wait!"

cried Freddy, as he followed his friends.
He waddled along and jiggled his flippers.
The cliff edge came closer and
closer and then...

... "Stop!"

cried the flying instructor.

"You...

... can't...

... fly!"

It was **too late.**
Freddy dropped like a rock...

... **splosh,**

into the sea.

On the shore, everyone burst out laughing.
"It's a **sea monster!**" they cried.

Freddy squelched off, all by himself.
"I'll **learn** how to fly," he muttered.
"Just you wait and see."

That afternoon, in Freddy's house, there was a mysterious clattering and banging and tapping. Everyone wondered what was going on.

"I've made my own wings!"
cried Freddy. "I'm ready to fly!"

Lenny and Flo tried to tell Freddy that he
couldn't fly but Freddy wouldn't listen.

Even though Freddy flapped
and flapped, the result was
always the same.

Bang!

Wallop!

"You've got to face it," said Lenny and Flo.
"You just can't fly."

Bang!

crash!

Tap-tap!

That afternoon, on the ice, there
was even more mysterious crashing
and banging and tapping.

"We've made you a plane!" cried Lenny and Flo.
Freddy climbed on-board. "We're cleared for take-off,"
said the flying instructor. "Hold on tight. Here we go."

The gulls all **pulled** and tugged.

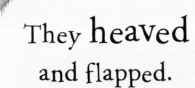

They **heaved** and flapped.

Suddenly, the little plane began to **move**.

"Wheeeeeee! "I'm flying!"

cried Freddy.

The little plane looped and swooped.
It dipped and dived.

Then, suddenly, Freddy's tummy felt funny.
It began to rumble and grumble.
He felt queasy and dizzy. "I don't like flying,"
said Freddy. "I feel sick."

"Emergency landing!"

cried the flying instructor.

The birds swooped to land, but the little plane swerved.
It skidded and flipped and everyone tumbled into a tangle.
Freddy and his friends had landed on Penguin Island.

"Everyone looks exactly like me!" cried Freddy.
"That's because **you're a penguin.**"
replied Lenny and Flo.

The penguins were
very friendly.

"We're good at diving," they said.
"Do you want to see?"
"Yes, please!" cried Freddy.

"We're good swimmers, too," said the penguins
and they whizzed,

splosh!

into the water.

"**Wow!**" cried Freddy.
"That looks **much** more fun than flying!"

All afternoon, the penguins and the gulls played together. They **paddled** and **dived**. They swooped and looped. They splished and splashed. Freddy was **happy** again. It didn't matter that he couldn't fly. It was pretty cool being a penguin! He'd had an adventure and found lots of new friends.

For Freddy, today was definitely
the best day, ever!

"Goodbye,
See you soon!"